"In a time of deceit, telling the truth is a revolutionary act."

-George Orwell

The Scarab of Truth

by Brett J. Baker

THE SCARAB OF TRUTH

ISBN: 979-8-847120-71-5

A Royal Crown Press Book
royalcrownpress.com

Cover Illustration and Design by Brett J. Baker

Chapter 1

The Offer

THE SCARAB OF TRUTH

Life on the fringe can be hard. It can be very, very hard.

The galactic rim, otherwise known as "the fringe" is a rough-and-tumble, anything-goes sort-of place. Worlds out here tend not to be as rich in resources, and neither do the people. In fact, if I were to summarize the people who live out here, it would be desperate.

At best fringer tech is going to be 25 to 50 years old, and even then, somebody's probably going to be looking to steal it from you, take it from you, or worse kill you for it. Nope, living on the fringe is not the easy life. Not. At. all.

My name is Tristain Varix. I'm a human. Of course, Varix wasn't originally my family's surname. I changed it because I didn't want to be associated with what my family did in the past. See, there aren't very many of us left these days. A while back, maybe a century or more, those of us who could afford to leave our homeworld on Earth did so and blasted off into space. We had to because... well... we couldn't stay. Our planet was burning up. It was a self-inflicted wound, you see. Greed. Greed made us do it... well not all of us, but certainly the ones in charge, the ones who could afford to build or otherwise buy a ship, or buy passage on a ship. We left the rest there on Earth to die on a planet that was growing more and more inhospitable every year. We even went so far as to forget where we left it. You read that right, we "lost" the coordinates to our former homeworld as if forgetting the Earth could somehow make us forget what we did there, and the billions who died. Not our greatest moment. But did we learn from our mistakes? Of course not. We thought we would find another home somewhere else and use that one up too. How stupid we were. Now pretty much every other species in the galaxy despises us because we happily set about despoiling every world we land on and we dump our garbage everywhere. The Pharoanic Confederation even declared us a blight upon the galaxy and initiated a war of extermination that wiped out the half-dozen or so colonies we tried to establish after leaving Earth. Maybe they're right. Maybe they did a service for the rest of the galaxy by wiping all but the last few of us out, but let me tell you, I am sure getting tired of being despised by everybody I run across. Sometimes I wish I could go back in time to those idiots who made the Earth into a hotbox and...

Well no words can really describe what I would do, but the way I see it, the plight of what's left of our species is all their fault. Least they're dead now.

And me? What about me you ask? I lucked out. I guess I've always been kind of lucky. A few years back I swindled a Kemettha noble out of his ship in a game of Ashok. Ashok is like a card game with hieroglyphs where... you know, it's not important. The ship, the *Menuqet* is a Pharoanic Starhawk, registered inside the Confederation, which gives me the ability to go anywhere, even into Confederation space. That landed me a job with KoloaCorp a fringe corporation that hired me on as a surveyor. The Kivaarians who run KoloaCorp might be about the only people in the galaxy who would hire a human. They honestly don't care who I am or where I come from as long as I keep bringing them back coordinates for resources they can harvest...

"What kind of trouble are you stirring up now meat-sack?" said the big, red, broad-shouldered, bipedal alien with the head of a catfish. He was dressed in tan coveralls bearing a KoloaCorp patch on the shoulder that matched the one on my jacket as he came over and sat down next to me with a drink.

"Shut up fish-face, can't you see I'm writing?" I responded. His name is Torgo. He's what's called a Callirrhoan, and his people were once slaves of the Confederation. He is my crew on the *Menuqet*, and also my best friend.

"Writing," he repeated in a derisive tone. "Why would you waste your time with that? If you want to keep a journal just use the holorecorder like everybody else."

"Would you leave me alone?" I replied, my eyes locking onto his. The barbels around his mouth twitched.

Torgo took a gulp of some viscous orange liquid that smelled suspiciously like cough syrup. "Fine, waste your time. It's not like anybody will ever read what you're writing. I mean, it's only the precious moments of your life tick-ticking away…"

"God you are so annoying when you drink," I responded. Then I swiveled in my seat and turned my back to him, shifting the holographic keypad that had been hovering in front of me, and the floating composition of words over about 90 degrees to be as far away from Torgo and his illiterate hate as possible.

But no sooner did I get the idea of what to write next, than did I sense more than see a big, bulky figure approaching.

It was a Krog. A big, lumbering, ugly sucker with grey skin and red eyes, his mouth twisting into a naturally hateful scowl. I had never seen him before in my life, and yet he stomped straight up to me. "Out of the way Earth monkey!" He shoved me into Torgo, and made a point of occupying the spot where I had been sitting, even though there was plenty of empty space at the bar.

"Hey!" Torgo shouted, rising to his feet.

The big Krog turned, red pupils burning from red corneas beneath his granite grey brow, his head rising to a crest that ran from the top of his head down the back of his neck. He was dressed head to toe in black leathers.

"I have no problem with you, Callirrhoan," the Krog said, his gravelly voice booming from within the cavernous void of his massive chest.

Torgo made a point of stepping into the sitting Krog, and he tilted his head as it drew close. "Well if you have a problem with my friend here, then I have a problem with you. Now I suggest you vacate that seat and move on before this gets ugly."

The Krog sneered and growled. Maybe it was the tilt of Torgo's head, the look in his eye or the stubborn set of his jaw, but he rose, standing a couple of inches taller than my fish-headed friend. "Are you going to step aside so I can vacate, or are we going to do this?"

Hearing this, Torgo stepped aside. The Krog shot me a murderous glare then lumbered away.

Torgo returned to his seat, and I returned to mine.

"Thanks," I said. "I take back everything I just said about you."

"Tristain, Tristain," Torgo replied, "Where would you be without me?"

"I'm sure I would be ruling my own private world somewhere standing atop a mountain wearing sun god-like robes as thousands of sex-starved women swarm all over themselves just trying to get a fleeting touch of me."

Torgo laughed. "In your dreams. The reality is somebody probably would have eaten you by now."

"That probably *is* the more likely scenario," I conceded.

"That was very exciting," somebody new said as they approached. I turned and saw a Kemettha. The Kemettha are very much like humans, but with two key differences, first, they are completely unable to grow hair of any kind, and second they have natural dark markings around their eyes that are pretty much identical to how the ancient Egyptians used to decorate their eyes. it was like some kind of natural tattoo or something. The Kemettha were probably the most populous species in the galaxy and they were also the species that ruled the Pharoanic Confederation. In short, they enjoyed such hegemonistic power, that they were virtually able to go anywhere without having to worry about negative consequences, because nobody wanted the wrath of the Confederation to come back onto them.

"You are human," the Kemettha observed as he sidled up to us. I looked at him. He was pale and bald, wearing a wide golden collar decorated with lapus lazuli and ruby ornamentations, He also wore a fine linen tunic and skirt, a golden belt, and golden sandals again decorated with lapus and rubies. Here before us stood a man whose garments could feed us both for 5 years if we were to sell them on the black market.

"That's me," I responded. "Just a great big brimming bunch of human."

"I come with a proposition," the Kemmetha said. "My name is Kauket. I represent a certain individual of status and power who has an interest in finding Earth."

I turned and looked at this Kemettha named Kauket. "Maybe you haven't heard, but we forgot where Earth is about a hundred years ago, give or take..."

"Yes," Kauet replied. "however, I believe you can find it again. I can offer you 250,000 Pharoanic Credits."

My eyebrows went up as I heard the amount. I turned and looked over at Torgo. He looked just as shocked.

"I'm sorry," I replied as I turned back to face Kauket again. "How much did you say?"

"Two hundred and fifty thousand," Kauket repeated more slowly. "I imagine it would be enough for your Callirrhoan friend here to climb into a bottle of Sovarian Ambrosia and never come back out."

As an aside, just so you're aware, 250,000 Pharoanic Credits is *a lot* of money. It's not quite buying your own private moon kind of money, but it's getting there. Okay, back to the story.

"I'm guessing that your employer, this 'individual of status and power' must *really* want to find Earth if he's willing to pay that much," I began.

Kauket's brow creased. "Yes…" he responded, not sure where I was taking to conversation.

"I mean, don't get me wrong," I continued, "I'm certainly interested in the offer but…"

"But…" Kauket echoed, sensing a point was fast approaching.

"I want to know what we're getting into," I said. "Afterall, it's not like offers for a quarter mil are raining from the sky. Your employer must be looking at some real trouble if he's willing to pay this much."

Kauket smiled. It was the smooth, smarmy smile of a schemer. His chin jutted out toward me as his head tilted back. "you mistake my employer's generosity for desparation, Mister…"

"Varix," I responded. "Tristain Varix, and my apertif-guzzling friend here is Torgo." Torgo nodded at the Kemettha and Kakuet's smile took on a little bit of awkwardness for just a moment.

"Let's just say that a good portion of what you are being paid for is discretion, Mr. Varix," Kauket replied. "That means no questions will be asked, and no answers will be given."

"Then I am afraid we have no deal, Mr. Kauket." I responded.

His eyes grew wide and he stared at me in disbelief. "Wh-what?"

"See, the way I figure it, you *need* to find Earth, and you need to find it fast. Why else would you be looking for a human to reconstruct its location? But there aren't a lot of us around are there? In fact, I'll wager you knew I was going to be here didn't you? I can take it even one step further and surmise that I am probably the first human you have ever met, am I right? Of course I am. You come to me offering me enough money to be able to live comfortably somewhere for the rest of my life, and you think I'll be just stupid enough to take the offer without finding out what the danger involved is? Do I look stupid to you Mr. Kauket? Of course I don't, so here's the deal. You tell me what the risk is, and I might take your offer. If you don't then I surely won't and you can try to find some other human wandering around out here stupid enough or wet behind the ears enough to go for walking into a dangerous situation completely blind. Savvy?"

Kauket looked down at the floor and shook his head. "Very well," he said. "My master is Pharoah of a member of the Pharoanic Confederation…"

"I guessed as much," I interjected.

"He has a slave who has escaped him and stolen one of his ships. She is determined to find Earth. You see, there are rumors that there was once an artifact hidden there in the Great Library of Alexandria."

"But the great library was destroyed by the Romans in 48 B.C.E.," I replied.

"Yes," Kauket replied, "but likely not all of it. As I'm sure you're already aware, the kingdom you knew as Egypt actually began as a Pharoanic colony, and we remained active in Egypt for much of its history. *We* had a hand in building the library, and *we* built a vault beneath it."

My eyes lit up. "Now you have my attention. What's the artifact? And how do we get into the vault?"

Kauket's eyes narrowed on me. "I must make it clear to you that at the end of this commission, my master must have possession of the artifact, or there will be no payment."

I rolled my eyes. "Fine," I conceded. "What's the artifact."

"A golden amulet… of a winged scarab below a solar disk," Kauket said.

"You Pharoanics and your scarabs," I replied. "And how do we get into the vault?"

"Not even I know that," Kauket responded. "But the clock is ticking. We suspect that my master's slave is already on the surface of Earth looking for the vault."

"What can you tell me about this slave then?" I asked.

"Her name is Nephthesit. She is smart, and resourceful, but otherwise unremarkable."

I looked sideways at him. He wasn't telling me everything about this Nephthesit. But if she was already on-world, then the clock really *was* ticking…

"Alright Mr. Kauket, we'll take your deal," I said.

"I must emphasize, my employer is paying you to locate the planet only. Do not interfere. When you find earth, send the coordinates to this holocom frequency," he said as he swiped his two fingers on his left hand toward me and a hologram of a set of letters and numbers shot over toward me, coming to rest right in front of me. "We will do the rest," he finished.

"Find the planet, send you the coordinates, get paid," I summarized, "got it."

"Very good," Kauket finished with a nod. "Send your account information to that frequency, and we will pay you as soon as we have the coordinates."

"Will do," I replied.

Kauket nodded to us both, then he got up and turned to leave, but he paused and then turned back to face us.

"You know, you are very much not what I expected," Kauket began. "I had your people were of low intelligence, and that they didn't have much awareness of the consequences of their actions. I am pleased to learn that you are one of the good ones. Good day, Mr. Varix."

As he walked away, I turned to Torgo.

"One of the good ones?" I repeated in a low tone, "can you *believe* that guy?"

Chapter 2
The Lost World

"What a bit of luck!" I said to Torgo as we left the bar weaving our way across Varico Station toward the docking bays. "This job will pay us both enough to be able to retire in comfort. We won't either of us be wealthy, but we'll both be well-off!"

"And all we have to do is find Earth," Torgo said as he lumbered beside me, then fell back behind so we could navigate our way through a tight passage between onrushing people. "How are we going to do that? I hope you have an idea."

"I do," I said back over my shoulder. "The *Menuqet* is patched into the Confederation's unimatrix."

"The what?" Torgo asked in reply.

"The unimatrix," I said again. "It's a huge network of Confederation supercomputers that contain the totality of all knowledge compiled by the Kemettha. No doubt that's how our fugitive slave girl found Earth. Lucky for us, neither Kauket or his boss thought to look for it there."

"Or *knew* to look there," Torgo replied as he caught up and was walking at my side again. "What makes you think you will find the location of Earth there?"

"Uh… like Kauket said, the Kingdom of Egypt was actually a colony, originally," I replied in a tone of voice meant to convey that what I was saying should be obvious.

"Hmph," Torgo responded. "Frankly, I'm surprised you took the job. Helping Kemettha pharoahs retrieve their runaway slaves doesn't really seem like our style. And then there's the whole bounty hunter thing…"

"What bounty hunter thing?" I asked.

"Why didn't Kauket hire professional bounty hunters to bring her back?" Torgo observed.

"Who better to find Earth than a human?" I replied. "Besides, any bounty that is captured would have to be reported to the Fugitive Recovery Authority… and then there would be a record…"

"Exactly!" Torgo responded. "There's something here that pharoah is trying to keep hidden by keeping this off the books.

"I mean, if I were Callirrhoan, I might think everything smells fishy too but..."

"Very funny, fleshmonkey!" Torgo objected. "But seriously, don't you suspect something here is off?"

"I always suspect something's off," I replied. "I just expect I'll figure a way to come out ahead anyway."

"Yeah, the thing about being lucky," Torgo began, "is that you don't want to be stuck standing around like a moron when it runs out."

I had a witty reply locked and loaded, but I let it drop as I spied the *Menuqet* moored to its docking terminal. "There's the ship," I said.

She was a golden-sheened beaut. Wide, sweeping curved wings spread out from either side of the sleek body of the ship forming a crescent moon that was fashioned into even segments to resemble the wing feathers of a hawk. The main body narrowed at the front into a beak-like point that curved downward, and in the rear were two banks of powerful propulsion engines flanking the warp drive, which protruded back at the center under the tail which was again segmented to resemble tailfeathers. Of course, as this was not a military vessel, but rather, a personal barge, the only weapons aboard were ones I had made modifications to mount under its wings… a pair of Mark 20 plasma repeater cannons. But what she lacked in punching power, *Menuqet* more than made up for with superior speed and maneuverability. I was fairly confident that if it ever hit the fan, I could probably count the ships in the galaxy that I couldn't outrun on one hand, and even those ships, I could make look foolish by outflying them.

As we boarded, Torgo and I headed toward the front for the bridge. I took my usual seat at the pilot's station, and he sat in his traditional seat at the co-pilot's station. With a sweep of my hand, I brought up the ship's full suite of holomenus. Admittedly, the link to the unimatrix's holographic user interface wasn't one that either of us accessed frequently… okay fine it wasn't one that either of us had accessed *ever*.

"Unimatrix online," the interface said as a series of holomenus opened up all around me.

"Unimatrix," I began, "please display coordinates of the planet called Earth."

"Coordinates not available," the Unimatrix responded.

"Interesting," Torgo replied.

"Unimatrix," I continued, "Why are the coordinates not available?"

"Coordinates for the Sol system were sealed by order of the Pharoanic Council after the withdrawal of the Confederation from its colony on planet Earth in the year 24667 P.Y."

"Well this is unexpected," I said turning to Torgo.

"Look who thinks he's so smart now," Torgo replied with a snide little smile. "I'm dying to see how you come out on top this time."

"Shaddup," I replied. Then I turned my attention back to the array of holomenus arranging themselves around me. "Unimatrix, calculate the Pharoannic year 24667 into Earth's Julian calendar. What year was that?"

"48 B.C.E.," the unimatrix replied.

"Same year the Romans burned the great library to the ground. Tensions would escalate between Cleopatra and Marc Antony on one side, and Augustus on the other until war broke out between them in 32 B.C.E., and eventually Egypt would be conquered by the Romans in 30 B.C.E. after the deaths of Antony and Cleopatra."

"So what other clues do we have?" I continued, thinking out loud. "Unimatrix, tell me about the Scarab amulet believed to be buried below the library of Alexandria."

A holographic image of a golden scarab with wings spreading out on either side of it as it reached for a solar disk that rested above it appeared, rotating in the air before me. "The sacred scarab of Pharazon. Long sought after as the missing piece of the royal regalia of the first pharoah, the sacred scarab was also called the 'scarab of truth,' as it was rumored to grant visions to those seeking the truth,"

"The scarab originally rested atop the sarcophagus of Pharazon at the heart of his great pyramid, but robbers broke into the pyramid in 24039 P.Y. The scarab was believed to have been reclaimed in 24664 P.Y. by the newly-crowned Queen Cleopatra, who ordered it sealed into the vault beneath the great library of Alexandria at the insistence of representatives of the Pharoanic Council. It is still believed to reside within the vault to this day."

"What was the council playing at by sealing the coordinates, effectively making it impossible for them to reclaim it, I wonder? It's almost like they didn't want it to be found."

Torgo nodded. "And remember how defensive Kauket got when you expressed an interest in reclaiming the scarab?"

"Yeah," I responded. "He shut me down."

"Exactly," Torgo said. "It's called the scarab of truth. I wonder what truth Kauket and his employer are trying to hide?"

"Makes me wonder if it was really the Romans who burned the library," I replied.

"But we still don't know where Earth is," Torgo countered.

"I'm working on it, okay?" I shot back. "Unimatrix, Tell me about Pharazon."

An image of a tall, broad-shouldered man in a nemes headdress appeared, and started to rotate before me. "Pharazon was the first pharoah of Kemet, homeworld of the Kemettha. During his lifetime, he built an empire encompassing 80 nearby worlds. Upon his death in 376 P.Y. he was worshipped as a God as he was sealed into his tomb in the Great Pyramid of Pharazon on Kemet. In the aftermath of his passing, his empire broke up into rival Pharoanic states, which led ultimately to the formation of the Pharoanic Confederation in 507 P.Y. In 788 P.Y. the Forum of the Prophets that to this day serves as the meeting place for the

Pharoanic Council was built. Its location was chosen because of its proximity, and the direct line of sight that it enjoys to the Great Pyramid."

"Pharazon was also the founder of the art form known as Astromancery, and was said to be highly adept at accessing the astrum in order to alter the shape of reality. He wrote multiple treatises on Astromancery that are all kept under guard and tightly controlled by the Academy of astromancery."

"Okay, our runaway slave found the coordinates of Earth somehow," I observed out loud. "How did she do it?"

"Unimatrix," I continued, tell me about the great library of Alexander.

Then an image popped up of a tall lighthouse with a fire burning atop it jutting out into a harbor from the coastline. Behind stood a complex of hellenistic buildings stretching out across a sizeable campus. The buildings were all decked with vaulted rooftops, tall colonnades, and lavish sculptures. "The Great Library of Alexandria was the most famous library on Earth during the classical period. Although there is some debate over the date, it is believed to have been built in 24432 P.Y. by Ptolemy I Soter, founder of the Ptolemaic Dynasty that ruled Egypt from 24410 P.Y. until 24685 P.Y. At its height, the library was said to contain anywhere from 400,000 to 700,000 scrolls and parchments in addition to works of art, sculptures, maps, and other works." Several other images popped up on either side of the image of the library, which was spinning slowly. But one of the images caught my eye. I touched it with both hands, and spread them, expanding the image. It appeared to be a map painted onto a vaulted ceiling... a star map. And what was that star I spied at its center? Sol! That was the location of Earth!

This was it! This image was how she found Earth! "Well would you look at that?" I said. Torgo got to his feet and his eyes narrowed as he peered at the image. "If we know the stars that surround it, then we can calculate the location!"

It took us several more hours to translate the names of the stars surrounding Sol, but eventually we worked up a working star map. We were surprised to find that Earth, and most of the stars in this sector of space lay outside what was currently considered known space. It made me wonder if the

Confederation had overreached in founding a colony on Earth, or if its borders had shifted over the centuries? There had been several wars with competitors in that region in the centuries since they withdrew.

Once we had our map worked out, we disembarked from Varico station, and made our way out toward the outer system until we were confirmed to be at a safe distance.

"Shall we go have a look?" I asked Torgo.

He nodded back. "Let's go see if we were right."

I pulled the lever that controlled the warp drive down on the console toward myself, and there was a deep bass hum that began building up as the warp drive pulsed to life. Soon we could hear it oscillating, and as it continued we could see the familiar warping of reality taking shape in front of the nose of our ship into a bowl-shaped depression. Of course, both Torgo and I knew well that while gravity and mass were being manipulated at the front of the ship so was it also being manipulated behind the ship, pressing timepsace up behind us.

Then, when timepsace had warped around us enough to become supercharged, there was a sound of energetic whooshing as our ship started forward, slowly at first, not much faster than the speed of normal propulsion. But soon that inertial charge built up appearing like lightning that danced out from the tip of the Starhawk's beak and flickered as it licked and caressed the outer hull of the ship. Within just a few short moments, the outer planets were shooting past like a blur and then the oncoming stars of interstellar space just appeared as streaks as it almost seemed like time and space and reality all merged and became one distorted jumble with each moment seeming to merge together into an instantaneous eternity that felt like it could end in the mere blink of an eye.

In my mind I knew that the science of this meant we were utilizing the very forces that allowed universal expansion that exceeded the speed of light to travel well beyond that cosmological speed limit, but in that distorted moment that seemed both infinitesimally short and endlessly eternal at the same time, I lost that thought like a bird attempting to take flight and then getting itself sucked away into the maelstrom of cosmological forces that were raging all around us.

Then suddenly, we arrived, and our beautiful and terrible momentum stopped just like that, leaving all reality seemingly thundering in our ears and fading off into the distance across the great verge of timespace as it spread out away from us in all directions.

I shoved my pinky into my ear and wiggled it back and forth as I shook my head, manually adjusting the pressure of my eardrums as I tried to recover. It was the disorientation that followed from warping that was the worst. It was always the disorientation, and it took us both a few minutes for our minds to clear and our bearings to return.

"That never gets old," Torgo sarcastically grunted more than said.

"Right?" I replied. I blinked and suddenly, the memory of where we were going returned to me. I started looking around, and I spotted a yellow gas giant nearby with a breathtaking set of rings around it.

"It's Saturn!" I said, my eyes wide with wonder. "Torgo! We did it! We found Earth!"

Chapter 3
The Slave Girl

We had found Earth. I loaded up the holocom code, and sent off the signal to Kauket. But as soon as the signal had been sent, I became keenly aware of Torgo's eyes on me.

"What?" I asked.

"Just feels... *wrong* to me, you know?" Torgo replied. "Why are we turning a runaway slave back over to the people she escaped from?"

"I can think of 250,000 reasons why we're doing that," I replied.

"C'mon Tristain," Torgo shot back, "playful banter aside, is this really who we want to be? The Kemettha enslaved my people, just like that girl down there, and they declared your people a plague, and all but exterminated them. Why are we soiling our hands with their filthy blood money?"

Then a holo notification popped up in front of me, letting me know that 250,000 Pharoanic Credits had been deposited into my account.

I looked down at the holocontrols, which were essentially a pair of hovering holographic handbars surrounded by holographic sensor rings that surrounded my hands and tracked their movement, adjusting the ship accordingly. And as I sat there for just the briefest instant, I found my hands wanting to pilot the ship forward... toward Earth.

Why? I asked myself. Why would I want to do that? Was it because deep down in my black whithered heart I knew that Torgo was right?

"I just know I'm going to regret this," I said as I extended my arms, pushing both my hands out and away from myself. The ship responded by flying forward toward the inner solar system.

We approached that familiar blue orb, surrounded by a cloud of space debris; mostly crumbling satellites that still had yet to have their orbits decay. It's like: Hey, there's life that lives here, and we like to build a lot of stuff, but we never really learned how to clean up after ourselves... and we're coming to your world next. It's no wonder we were never visited by extra-terrestrials. Afterall, who would want to visit that neighbor who doesn't pick up his trash? But you already know my feelings on the matter, so I digress…

"Scanning the planet for lifeforms," Torgo said as he manned the ship's sensory console.

"Find anything?" I asked.

"I have one lifeform," Torgo replied, his eyes fixed on the hologram that hovered before him with a holographic beacon flashing before his eyes.

"Good," I replied. "We'll zero in on her coordinates, find her, warn her that Kauket is on his way, and hopefully get out of here while the Kemettha are none the wiser."

"You're doing the right thing Tristain," Torgo responded.

"Yeah," I chirped back. "Let's hope that right thing doesn't cost us our payment, or even worse… get us killed."

I brought the ship down, descending through the cloud of space junk into the upper atmosphere, then down even further until the ground was approaching us from below.

"What's the atmosphere like outside?" I asked.

"Hot..." Torgo replied. "Unbearably hot, and dry."

"Right," I said as I set the ship down in the sands, got up from my seat, grabbed my gun belt with my holstered blaster pistol from where it hung on the bulkhead beside me, and strapped it around my waist. "So, a hostile environment again. Should be nothing new for us. Don't forget your hydropack this time."

Torgo slung his blaster rifle over his shoulder so that it hung behind his back. Then as if to show me, he held up a small plastic pack filled with water. A tube and a mask hung from it that would allow him to breathe air artificially replicated to resemble a high-moisture atmosphere. Without it, he would pass out from dehydration after about 5 minutes in dry conditions like these.

He strapped the mask to his jawline sealing it tight over his mouth, and clipping the plastic pack to his belt as he followed me off the ship. The hatch closed rapidly behind us as we disembarked. It was like we had stepped out from a cool, air-conditioned ship's cabin into a sweltering oven. The heat literally felt like it was pressing against me, sucking the moisture from my skin. The air felt thick and hot in my lungs, and if I were to allow myself to panic, I might think I was going to suffocate from it, but I had years of practice handling weird atmospheric variations like this. We stood in a ruined city with the wind blowing dust in on us from the polar north. There was a platform before us, with a walk that jutted out a few meters. It very much reminded me of the image of the library of Alexandria.

"These must be the ruins of the lighthouse," I said, "which would mean that the library..."

I turned and pointed toward a tall colonnaded wall that very much resembled the first building on the library campus. With Torgo following behind, we made our way toward the ruined wall, the sand crunching beneath our feet as we went.

I was amazed to see how different everything appeared from the image I had seen. In that image the sky had been a rich shade of light blue, there were blue shimmering seas and grass so green one could almost feel its wet touch as it tickled the underside of one's bare feet. Here, there was no sea to be seen in any direction; the sky was an oppressive burnt orange with banks of clouds rolling across the horizon, thunder and lightning booming within their bowels. It was hot, and dry, and miserable, and the sand worked its way into everything, making one itch all over. The sooner we found the way down to the vault where no doubt, our slave girl was, the better off we would all be.

"Let's get a sensor scan of the campus," I said to Torgo, "see if we can find the way down that way."

But of course, the scan revealed nothing. However we were supposed to get down to that vault, it was well hidden.

So we searched… and we searched… *and we searched.*

"Tristain!" Torgo called after a good long time of searching, "Over here!"

I hurried over. He had found it. What appeared to be an old well with a cover that made the well appear to have been capped turned out to have a ladder of steel handlebars built into the side of a metal shaft leading down.

Clever girl, I thought as I climbed into the shaft, and began my descent. Even with no indication that anybody had followed her, she still had the sense to cover her tracks by putting the cover back on.

We made our way down into what was a large underground complex. There was a wide opening into the next chamber on our left, and a pale light flickered through from beyond. We could hear movement that way.

I looked up at Torgo who climbed down after me, and placed my forefinger across my lips in the universal gesture for him to shut the hell up with his loud climbing.

Stealthily, we reached the floor and crept forward. The chamber beyond was a perfectly round room cut from the earth and then walled in with perfectly placed blocks of stone. The vault itself was also round and occupied the center of the room, which made the outer chamber into a donut-shaped circle that surrounded it on all sides. We had no idea what lay on the other side of the room beyond the vault, but we could see the slave girl's silhouette in the midst of the flickering light and the long shadows they cast.

As we grew closer, her features became more visible through the dim light. She was completely bald like all Kemettha, and she was of a slight build with slender hips. She wore some coarse linen garment that looked like it might have been sackcloth or burlap; it covered her shoulders, torso, midsection, hips, and pelvis. She looked like she was busily trying to jury-rig something, and hadn't seen us yet.

"Excuse me," I said as I approached. She looked up at me with the most striking blue-green eyes I had ever seen. Her skin had a tannish-brown complexion to it. She had upswept almond-shaped eyes with the usual ornamental decorations surrounding them, and a slightly upturned nose that seemed to draw her upper lip into a natural, pouting curl. For just a moment, I couldn't help but be taken in for just an instance by the beauty of her face. Then I had to remind myself that I had no idea how old this slave girl actually was.

Seeing us approach, she shot up to her feet and started to back away from us toward the vault door behind her. It was a towering pair of steel doors latched together with a large wheel crank at the center which operated the mechanism that would cause the door to open.

"Miss," I said, "We are not your enemies, we're not here to hurt you. We've come to warn you. Do you know a Kemettha named Kakuet?"

"Kakuet," she repeated with a frown as her brow furrowed. "I would spit at the mention of his name… if I had any spit to give."

"He's coming here," I said. "Whatever this is you're trying to do, you will need to leave it behind and get out of here. He will be here shortly!"

"I am not leaving without the scarab!" she replied.

"Why?" I asked. "What's so special about it that you would risk your newfound freedom to claim it?"

"Who are you?" she asked. "How do you know me? Do you know who Kakuet serves? Do you know who *I* really am?"

I spread my hands out placatingly toward her. "That's a lot of questions all at once," I replied. "My name is Tristain Varix, and this is Torgo. We're surveyors. We were hired by

Kakuet to find this planet. But I wouldn't take the job until he told me why he wanted to find it. He said he wanted to reclaim an escaped slave. I assume by that he means you. Torgo and I are risking our commission to warn you so you can get away..."

"I will *not* leave without the scarab," she repeated.

"Why not?" I asked.

"My name is Nephthesit," she answered. "I am the only child of Akhumet, Pharoah of Khalatet. Kakuet serves Ammon, my father's former Grand Vizier who betrayed him, overthrew his rule, and executed him along with my mother. Then Ammon made me his slave, and commanded that I provide him with an heir that night. They took all my clothes and possessions and gave me this to wear. The first thing I did was wept for my parents. Then I grew tired of weeping, and decided that if there is any justice to be had in this universe, I would find it for them. So, before Ammon arrived that evening to make use of his slave, I escaped. I stole his personal barge, and once I was able to decipher the location of this lost world, I came here. Now I have been here for almost a full day, but I have not been able to get past these doors and into the vault."

"Well time has almost run out," I said. "If you stay here, Kakuet will find you."

"I am *not* leaving without the scarab," she repeated again. "The Pharoanic Council is meeting on Kemet in 3 days. I need some way to discredit him before the council so that he will be removed from my father's throne."

"You're hoping that the scarab will grant you a vision because you seek the truth?" Torgo asked.

"Yes," Nephthesit said. "This was the only thing I could think to do. The only chance I have to see justice done for my parents."

I let out a tired sigh as my gaze shot to the floor and I shook my head. Was I really going to do this? Was I really going to fly in the face of my own self-interest to help this stubborn fallen princess I didn't even know? But the question I found myself asking was this: would I be able to live with myself if I didn't? "Alright, if you won't leave without the scarab, then I guess the only option we have is to help you get it, and hope we can get it fast enough so that we can still make our escape before Kakuet arrives. Will that be suitable to you Nephthesit?"

"Neph," she replied. "I am no longer a princess, so you may call me Neph."

As Torgo walked past us both and approached the vault doors to give them a closer look, I nodded to her in response, then my eyes scanned the supplies she had brought. She had a survival lantern, about a hundred small blue orbs with a red glow coming from within them, and a bunch of various gadgets and doohickeys, none of which I recognized.

"Where did you find this collection of junk?" I asked as my eyes scanned the gadgets, then my eyes went back to the small blue orbs, "and are those... *Tetronium?*"

"Some of it was in Ammon's barge. The rest I stole as I made my escape from the palace."

"I'm not even going to mention how bothered I am to see that pile of explosive orbs. What is that you're trying to jury rig?" I asked, gesturing at what was in her hands with a point of my chin.

"It's a digital scanner drone," she said holding up a flying robotic device that was inert in her hands. "I was trying to get it to do an infrared scan of the locking mechanism, but it appears to be broken."

"And what do we have for our 2200-year-old lock over there Torgo?" I called.

"Looks like a numeric lock," Torgo responded. "An infrared scan would have likely shown which buttons to push, then it would have been a matter of..."

"Trying all the combinations in turn," Neph finished.

"Exactly," Torgo responded with a nod. "Good call."

I walked over and squatted down on my haunches near the pile of Tetronium beads. figuring they might come in handy later, I grabbed up two handfuls and stuffed them into my pockets. "Lucky for you, the sensor arrays aboard the *Menuqet* come fully equipped," I replied.

"Already scanning," Torgo responded. Then he started pressing buttons on the lock, until there came a loud metallic clacking sound that filled the chamber, and then a hissing sound as oxygen from the chamber was vented into the pressurized vault.

"Well," I began as I got up, went over and stood next to Neph, "Let's see what this scarab that everybody makes such a big fuss over is all about, shall we?"

Torgo backed away from the doors as they very slowly began to swing open. Then as they parted, they revealed a relatively small chamber, only tall enough for a man of average height to stand inside, and only about as wide. Within was a single rather featureless looking pedestal, and there hovering above the pedestal was our golden scarab. We both drew closer and as we approached, we could see tiny rubies and lapus lazuli perfectly cut and meticulously set to add color and ornamental detail to the golden wings, which spread out straight from either side of the round body. A pair of small round ruby eyes were attached on either side of the head, and a large round, perfectly cut ruby had been placed into the solar disk as well.

"Huh," I remarked. "Considering all the bother, I expected the scarab to be more… *impressive*."

"Oh, but this is no ordinary scarab," Neph replied, "This was the missing piece of the Pharoanic regalia of Pharazon the great, the very first Pharoah."

"Yes, I'm aware," I replied as we both came and stood before the pedestal. "Well, would you like to do the honors?"

Neph reached out with both hands and touched the scarab. It almost seemed to respond to her impending touch by hovering toward her approaching hands as they drew close. Then she took hold of it.

"That's quite enough of that!" we heard an all too familiar voice call from the base of the shaft in the other chamber.

"Dammit!" I whispered to myself as we all turned to see Kakuet with a half dozen Pharonial soldiers wearing striped nemet headdresses of blue and gold, and armed with a type of polearm weapon that we out on the fringe referred to derisively as "zapsticks" because when they were used to fire blasts of plasma, they made a distinctive "zap" sound. Then emerging from the crowd to stand at the fore of the group was another figure. I could hear Neph inhale sharply, and I could literally feel her bristle as he approached.

He was fair-skinned, and broad-shouldered, with a well-toned muscled physique. He wore a golden skullcap and a postiche-styled metallic false beard. And in his eyes, I saw such malice.

"I am Ammon, Pharoah of Khalatet," he proclaimed, his deep voice booming as it echoed throughout the chamber. "You will return to me what is mine!"

Chapter 4
The False Pharoah

On the homeworld of my people, we used to have this saying: "all my chickens have come home to roost." Admittedly, I never really understood what that saying meant, but somehow in situations like this, it always seemed like a very appropriate thing to say.

Having now seen Ammon, I took an instant dislike to him, so I did what I always do when faced with an overweening antagonist that is bringing impossible odds to bear: I doubled down in the most obnoxious way possible.

Stepping to the fore opposite Ammon, I spread my arms wide and bowed at the waist. "Oh great and horny Pharoah of Khalatet," I called in an equally loud voice to counter Ammon's, "I Tristain Varix bid you greeting and welcome you to the lush tropical paradise of my homeworld, Earth."

I didn't even have to see the faces of the people around me to know their reactions. See, Torgo had seen me do this many times so right now he was rolling his eyes and shaking his head. Neph, meanwhile who was now standing a few steps behind me holding the scarab in her hand had a look of shocked confusion, like she was watching a train wreck happen right before her eyes. I always love that look, *especially* on her. Kakuet, hearing my words, likely wore a similar expression. The Pharonic soldiers they had brought, being completely mirthless individuals probably had more of a look of impatience. No doubt they wanted to kill us and get this confrontation over with so they could return to Khalatet and get back to busily slathering each other with tanning lotion prior to their usual *shenanigans*... or so I imagine...

But I didn't have to imagine Ammon's expression. My eyes were as fixed on him as my wide smile was fixed on my face. He glared at me like a man contemplating all the ways he could murder me for my impudence. This too was a look I knew well, because I had seen it pretty much my entire life.

"You simply must try the tropical drinks. The surf washing up on the shore and the cool breeze against your skin... these are the stuff of memories that will last a lifetime!"

"What are you jabbbering about you madman?" Ammon replied. "It's a godsforsaken desert hellscape out there, and there are no tropical drinks! You will cease your talking immediately or I will have your tongue removed and made into an ornament. And that *slave*," he continued, pointing at Neph, "will return with me and she will give me many fine sons and heirs to perpetuate my dynasty!"

"I would rather die!" Neph cried back.

"Trust, me you obstinate ungrateful woman, I can make that happen just like I did for your parents!"

Upon hearing those words, that was the moment I decided that this guy didn't just need to be denied his prize, he also needed to be embarrassed in the process.

"Ah, so she says she would rather die than let you lie between her legs, yet you insist nonetheless!" I interjected as I stepped in between pharoah and slave. "I'm pretty that is called rape regardless of what corner of the galaxy you happen to find yourself in."

Ammon pointed at me and he snarled as his dark eyes burned with indignity. He had clearly decided he'd had enough. "Kill them! Kill the human and the Callirrhoan and bring the slave and the scarab to me!"

Ammon's soldiers came surging forth like a swarm, lowering their zapsticks toward us...

"Time to go!" I cried as I grabbed Neph by the wrist, and we ran around the donut-shaped outer chamber, hoping beyond hope that there was a door on the other side.

"You know, just once I would like to get out of one of these situations *without* being shot at!" Torgo said as he came up running alongside us, beams of purplish plasma shooting past us on both sides.

"Me too, buddy," I responded. "Me too. I just can't help myself."

"Get therapy, Tristain," Torgo responded as another blast of purple-colored plasma whizzed past his head, "seriously!" He returned fire a couple of times with his blaster rifle.

We made it far enough around the circle to see what was on the other side from where we had been. Low and behold, there was another doorway leading to what appeared to be a darkened corridor beyond.

With the Pharoanic guards behind us firing blasts of plasma everywhere, we plunged through the doorway and into the darkened corridor, thankful that Ammon's soldiers were all terrible shots.

And no sooner had I finished thinking that then did one of the Pharoanic soldiers let loose a blast of purple plasma that caught Torgo in the back of one of his calves.

With a cry, he collapsed into the dirt, holding the back of his leg.

I looked back over my shoulder and I saw him fall and roll in the dirt with his leg elevated and in his grasp.

"Torgo!" I cried, as I stopped. I released Neph's wrist and then turned under heavy fire from Ammon's goons. Grabbing the front of Torgo's coveralls, I dragged him off toward one side. When Neph saw what I was doing she came and helped, holding the scarab with one hand, and helping to drag Torgo with the other. We got him safely into the opening of another entryway leading into a perpendicular corridor, all the while under continuous fire from the soldiers.

Then Neph set down the scarab beside us. Seeing the soldiers just about to reach the entryway into the corridor, she rose and raised her hands. She began to chant, and her voice took on a strange resonance that seemed to echo throughout reality all around us. Circular patterns of energy displaying sigils upon them emerged from her hands and then suddenly, there no longer was an entryway there that we had passed through. The guards were met with a solid wall instead.

Satisfied that the wall would hold them back, even if only for a few moments, she turned and knelt back down beside us.

"Let me see your wound," she said.

Torgo removed his hands from over where he had been shot. I winced as I saw it. It looked bad. Much worse than just a plasma burn. The flesh had been broken and penetrated into his bone. Seeing this as well, Neph chanted again. Her hands took on a green glow as a greenish light filled her eyes, then she touched the flesh around the wound. We all watched in wonder as the bone and flesh reformed while wound in his leg closed.

Within just a moment or two, we helped Torgo back onto his feet.

"The pain is gone!" he observed, his eyes wide with delight.

"Are you able to run?" I asked him.

Torgo responded with a nod.

"Then come on!" I said, as Neph grabbed the scarab again, and she and Torgo fell into step behind me. We retreated further into the network of criss-crossing corridors.

We ran for a good while, then we came to a large chamber with pillars, every inch of them covered with hieroglyphs. There was one pillar that had broken and fallen onto the floor. Neph went over and sat on the broken section of it to regain her breath.

"That thing you did back there," I asked, panting as Torgo bent down and grabbed his knees to get more air into his lungs, "what was that?"

"It's astromancy," Neph responded. "I am an astromancer."

"I've heard of that. Recently, I think…" I responded, trying to recall where I had heard it.

"It's not common," Neph responded. "It operates by accessing the astrum… the power of the astral realm to alter reality. Only a child of one of the 7 houses descended directly from Pharazon are able to practice it. Its secrets are tightly guarded by the houses and the academy."

"Impressive," I replied.

"I am grateful that you and your Callirrhoan friend came to warn me. I am sorry that I made you linger too long," Neph said. "Ammon, and those like him, they do not see me, they only see a receptacle for their seed… a womb. You were right to call him a would-be rapist."

"If I may ask," I responded, "How old are you?"

"19 standard pharoanic cycles." She replied.

"I wasn't sure. You appear younger, but the way you talk, how you carry yourself…"

"I have been raised to rule since I was old enough to walk, old enough to talk, old enough to read…" she responded. "I never really had a childhood to speak of."

"I'm so sorry you never got to be a child," I replied.

"It is my burden, and my sacrifice," she responded, her eyes going down to the scarab in her hands. "Once I discredit Ammon, I will return to Khalatet and assume my father's throne."

"I think you just might," I responded with a nod.

"That section of wall is not permanent," Neph said next. It will revert any moment now. We should continue to flee.

"I need another minute before we start running again!" Torgo interjected. "This dry air is murder, even *with* my hydropack."

My eyes went down to the scarab as well.

"I hope that thing is worth all this trouble," I said.

"So do I," she replied. "Pharazon too was an astromancer, like me. In fact, he was the *first* astromancer. Everything I learned, he first did. His texts and writings speak of this scarab. They state that truth is far more than we understand it to be."

"how so?" I asked.

"Truth is not simply a state of being true," Neph explained. "It is also the right action that follows it. Truth is by its very nature, a transformative power that brings change both to the holder of truth and the world around him. He that has truth but fails to act upon it betrays that truth and instead transforms himself into a living falsehood."

"So you're saying that truth isn't just about what is real, it's also about what you do with it?"

"Exactly," Neph responded. "The truth in the hands of one who is willing to unleash its full potential is a dangerous thing."

"My people had a saying: the truth will set you free."

"If your life is built on a foundation of truth, then indeed it will. But if your life has been built on falsehood, then truth will destroy you. That is why truth must be more than just what is spoken, it must be a *pursuit*."

"And you think that whatever is in this scarab will destroy Ammon?" I asked her.

"I know it will," she replied. "Whatsmore, he knows it too. That's why he fears it so. That's why he has come all this way."

"That's not the *only* reason," I replied. "He was pretty clear he wants you to have his children."

"Aside from him being a perverted narcissistic creep, he *needs* me to give his new regime in Khalatet legitimacy. The vast majority of the nobility were loyal to my father. If he does not have me by his side, then it becomes much more difficult for him to persuade them to play along."

"Ah, politics," I replied. "The science of forcing compromise so that nobody gets what they want and everybody is equally unhappy." With a gesture, I pulled up the sensory suite holomenu of the *Menuqet*.

"What are you doing?" she asked.

"I'm going to run a sensor scan to see if I can figure out how big this complex is down here. Maybe it will show us a safe place to hide from Ammon's stumblebums back there."

As the holographic layout was displayed spreading out across the available space, The three of us saw how vast this underground complex actually was.

"What's that there?" Torgo asked as he pointed to an area where the rooms were no longer perfectly cut from the underground stone, but rather seemed to have been formed naturally. There was a twisting passage that led down to a large room that was vaguely roundish in shape, and then up again where it rejoined a cut corridor that seemed to rise up to the edge of the map.

"It looks like a natural cave or tunnel of some kind," I observed.

"That is where we should hide," Neph offered. "Perhaps we might even find a way out."

With a swipe of my fingers, I shifted the whole map over so that area was before me. "It does look like you might be right. If these scans are correct; and mind you I can't imagine why they wouldn't be, this tunnel here seems to rise in elevation. It might be a passage back to the surface."

"Agreed then," Torgo added with a nod of certainty. "That's the way we should go."

Chapter 5

The Confession

We fled further into the underground complex, heading toward the caves. With this oppressive dry heat, Neph and I were both starting to feel parched. Of course, Torgo with his hydropack was still happy as a clam... the bastard.

We paused to rest, and I took out my cryothermic canteen, offering it first to Neph. She drank deeply.

"Thank you," she said, handing it back to me. "I had gotten pretty dehydrated."

I took a deep draught myself, then I put the cap back on and twisted it closed, which set the canteen into its chilling process. "There's still more if you need," I offered. Then I sat down next to her as Torgo stood nearby, keeping watch for pursuit from Ammon's goons.

"So what do you think *is* on that thing?" I asked, inclining my head toward the scarab. "What's Ammon really got to fear?"

Neph joined Torgo's gaze, looking off in the direction we had come for signs of pursuit. After a moment, when she was satisfied that they weren't hot on our heels, her teal-colored gaze went down to the scarab. "I suppose it couldn't hurt to take a peak and find out. However, Once I start pouring astrum into the scarab to gain access to what it carries... it will be difficult to extricate myself from it. You might need to protect me if Ammon or his guards arrive."

I drew my blaster pistol from where I wore it holstered on my hip. "I think Torgo and I can do that, can't we Torgo?"

Torgo looked at me and shook his head. "Your funeral," he replied.

Neph looked at us both wearing a quizzical expression, trying to understand the interaction.

"It's just this thing we do. It's called banter," I explained, my response shifting from Neph to Torgo, "and sometimes it's not entirely appropriate."

Torgo sighed and shook his head. "Don't worry kid," he said to Neph as he pulled the blaster rifle he carried slung behind his back, "we've got your back."

Neph nodded and repositioned herself so that she was sitting straight-backed with her legs folded beneath her. She placed the scarab in her lap, then she closed her eyes and began working through what seemed like a series of gestures. Before long, the familiar glowing rings and sigils appeared around her wrists and hands, and then the scarab seemed to take on an otherworldly glow as astrum began to pop and crackle forth from it.

And suddenly, there was another figure standing there in our midst. He had a bluish glow about him, and his figure was ghostly. Clearly this was an ancient hologram. This was an older man, in the last years of his life, dressed in regal pharoanic garb. He wore a metal postiche on his chin, and on his head was a pschent crown; the upper crown appearing lighter in color than the lower crown. He had a magnificent jeweled wide collar, and a golden belt with an ankh on it bound the linen kilt at his waist.

"I am Pharazon, ruler of Kemet, and I live in falsehood," He said. "I have created a society that is built on lies. I have profaned the faith of my people by subjugating it to political needs. In fact, I have politicized every aspect of our society, even our most sacred holidays. There is no corner of life that I have not left unturned. Such was my ambition to transform our society to see reality the way that I want them to see it. And many of my people believed my lies; they believed every word, and set themselves against those of my people who do not believe. But deep inside I know that they… that *we* have betrayed the truth to the point that we have lost sight of it altogether. Truth has decayed into nothingness to the point that now it is gone from us entirely, and I am to blame…"

I looked over at Neph and she looked back to me wearing a flabbergasted expression on her face. Obviously, she could not believe what she was seeing and hearing. Yet the hologram went on.

"Where simple political posturings were not enough, I constructed elaborate conspiracies that don't really exist. Where arguments failed, my followers became more extreme doubling down by making statements even they didn't believe in order to avoid conceding even a single point. The discourse of my time has descended into virtual anarchy. Those I have appointed to make laws have even overturned existing laws based on these false extremist views, and I am to blame. As a consequence of my lies, the astrum has all but left me. I have lost my astromancy. To you who view this, be warned and be wary, too much falsehood can have disastrous effects, and it can cause you to lose all that matters to you. Now I go to my tomb, having gained the pinnacle of worldly power, but having lost so much more to gain that power. Were I to have the same choice knowing what it would cost me... I would choose differently."

Then the hologram disappeared.

We sat in silence. For the Pharoanic Confederation, Pharazon was the key pivotal figure in their history. He was their unifier; the one who laid the groundwork for the founding of their hegemonistic interstellar coalition. And now we had just learned that he not only relied on deceit to build his empire, but that in his last days he had come to regret it. What did this mean? What would the implications of this revelation be?

"Can I see that?" I asked Neph as she sat there trying to digest what she had just seen. She handed the scarab to me.

I looked closely. This was not some ancient mystical relic from ages past that would prove indecipherable to any who did not practice astromancy as I had been led to believe as recently as even a few moments ago, but its construction *was* superior to any other recording device I had ever seen.

"This is an impressive piece of ancient tech," I said handing the scarab back to Neph, "but it is in fact a holographic recorder, and that was not a vision of the truth, that was an ancient hologram made by Pharazon in his last days. These visions that truth-seekers supposedly had must have been other holographic recordings stored in the device. I'm afraid it's a case of advanced technologies being mistaken for magic."

Now it was Neph who sat slack-jawed. "Do you realize what this means? The burden of responsibility that has just been placed upon our shoulders?"

"What burden?" I asked, my brow furrowing.

"He who holds the truth has a responsibility to it," Neph replied. "We have just learned that the entire Pharoanic Confederation was built upon a foundation of lies."

I thrust my hands out between us defensively. "Hey," I began, "hold on now!"

"I will *not* be made party to Pharazon's lies," Neph said. "This *must* be revealed!"

"Are you crazy?" I replied. "Something like this will get you killed! It could get *us all* killed!"

"You think I don't realize that?" Neph shot back. "You think I'm not scared? But this is so much bigger than me!"

I sighed and I shook my head. "Look, we can talk about this later. For now, let's just get moving again before Ammon's soldiers find us."

We ventured onward toward the caves in silence as we all became consumed with our own thoughts and fears.

We travelled down a long corridor until we arrived at the mouth of the caves, but then we saw something very strange beyond that opening. Something that really shouldn't have been there given the runaway dry heat of this world.

"Mist?" Neph said as she strode forward and reached her hand out toward it.

"How can there be mist here?" I wondered aloud. Is there a source of moisture nearby?

Neph reached out and closed her eyes, and the mist coiled around her fingertips like tendrils.

"This mist is not natural," she said. "It is fueled by astrum, I can feel it. It's not a source of moisture nearby, it is a boundary… a place where our realm and the astral realm draw near to one another… come."

I looked at Torgo and he wordlessly looked back at me and shrugged. We fell into step behind Neph.

"Tell us more about this astral realm," I said as we advanced into the cavern, and the mist swirled all around us, seeming to adapt to our presence as if it were somehow alive.

"It is a plane of spiritual being," Neph responded. "The place where the elements that make up our souls; the ka, the ba, and the akh travel to when we die. It contains all afterlives, all ideas, all dreams, all inspiration. As the old saying goes, the soul belongs to heaven, the corpse belongs to earth."

"So when you wield the power of the astral realm you are wielding the power of the afterlife?" I asked.

She stopped and smiled as she turned and faced us. "It is much more than that. The astrum is the power of death, yes; but it's also the power of life."

The pathway curved as it moved downward, deeper into the caverns. As we advanced, the path wound down through a big round chamber with natural stalactites and stalagmites that came together from ceiling and floor to form pillars at regular intervals along the walls. Between each pair of pillars on each side was an alcove where ghostly astral images of the Pharoanic gods seemed to hover motionless, except for their heads and their eyes. Their eyes seemed to follow us unceasingly as they watched our every move. In the center of the room, was a deep well of swirling, crackling energies, resting within a round pedestal of natural uncut stone. The air here had a strange electrical tingle about it that made the little hairs on the backs of our necks stand on end. In fact, this whole place felt sort of surreal, like we were somehow drunk on the otherworldliness of it.

"Have we crossed the boundary into the astral realm?" I asked aloud as we paused, looking around at the pillars and alcoves.

"I don't know," Neph replied. "What is this place?"

"It's almost like… some sort of gallery," Torgo offered.

Neph stepped in toward the well of energy resting within the uncut pedestal. As she drew close, she gasped. "It's astrum!" she said.

Then another ghostly image; another figure composed of crackling astrum appeared, approaching Neph from the other site of the well.

"Nephthesit, daughter of Akhumet, rightful heir of Khalatet," she said as she transformed into a diaphanous version of Neph herself, "Attend my words."

"But you're… *me*?" Neph asked.

"yes," the ghostly Neph answered. "I am. You carry in your hand the truth. You have 3 possible paths that are now open to you." The image of Neph offered her. "If you wish to see, then immerse your hand into the well, and I will show you."

Tentatively, Neph reached out, then recoiled for a moment.

"Neph don't!" I urged her.

"I must know!" she replied. Then again, she reached out her hand, and plunged it beneath the swirling surface of the astrum. Her form became frozen by the touch of the astrum, and her eyes became empty, as they were themselves filled with a white glow. Seeing this I ran up grabbing her by the shoulders. I meant to pull her away from the well, and detach her from the touch of the astrum, but instead, I too became frozen in place, and my eyes took on the same empty glow…

Chapter 6
The Three Paths

Everything rapidly faded to darkness as reality seemed to twist and shift all around her. When the darkness passed, and reality settled, Neph arrived in a darkened hall surrounded by wide pillars on either side that had been painted and carved with hieroglyphs covering virtually every inch of them.

She spied torches burning on the walls between the pillars providing faint light to the room. Up ahead, there was a raised dais. And upon that dais was a square wooden table with a golden scale upon it.

But it was the figure standing beside the table that gave her pause. He stood tall and lean, waiting patiently, wordlessly, his gaze was fixed on her unwaveringly.

He had the physique of a man, but the head of a jackal. He wore a wide golden collar, a linen kilt, and a golden belt with an ankh upon it. There could be no mistaking who he was. This was Anubis, the god of death.

"Am I..." Neph began as she stepped tentatively toward him, "Am I *dead*?"

Anubis silently nodded once in reply. He gestured for her to join him upon the dais before the square wooden table.

As she emerged onto the dais, she became aware of a second figure standing nearby, previously unseen. This figure she knew well. This figure she knew intimately. For this figure was also her, or rather the astral ghost version of her.

"Nephthesit, daughter of Akhumet, daughter of Haqikah, and deposed former heir of the throne of Khalatet," the ghostly, astral Neph called, "you will submit your heart to Anubis, and be judged."

Anubis approached her, towering over her. He had in one hand a feather, and with his other hand, he reached into her chest, and pulled out her heart. It sat dormant in his hand.

"Anubis will now weigh your heart against the feather," the other Neph explained as Anubis turned and placed both items onto the scale together. "The feather represents the truth. If the feather is heavier than your heart, then you shall be judged favorably. If your heart is heavier, then your judgment shall be unfavorable."

Neph held her breath as she, her other self, and Anubis all watched while her heart and the feather both took turns rising and falling on the scales. When finally, weight overcame inertia, It was the feather that rose, and her heart that lowered.

"What does this mean?" Neph asked as she stood there staring at her judgment, and became afraid.

"It means that you held the truth in your hands, but you betrayed it," the aetherial other Neph replied. "You discovered the scarab of truth, you viewed the confession of Pharazon, but chose not to reveal it. And so, you added your lie to his own, and that lie has weighed heavily upon your heart. Now, I am afraid, that the field of reeds is closed to you. You shall have to travel to the grey lands."

"What are the grey lands?" Neph asked. She literally could not stop her hands from trembling, she was so afraid.

"A landscape unchanging, uncompromising, and unsympathetic. Perhaps there you will learn the lessons you chose not to in this life. Perhaps you will learn to place a greater value upon the truth."

Then Anubis gestured silently behind the square table. There was a golden door on the far wall that hadn't been there before.

Neph swallowed, and her throat suddenly felt very tight. She was somehow compelled to walk forward. Her feet just started their advance toward the door on their own and as she drew near to the door, it swung open. Beyond she could see a cold, barren landscape below grey, placid, featureless skies.

And as she passed through the door, everything faded to black once more as reality twisted and sped off into the distance.

Suddenly reality seemed to snap into place all around her. Neph found herself lying in a bed in a strange room. She realized fairly quickly that this room very much reminded her of the bedroom shared by her parents in the Alabaster Palace on Khalatet, but the décor was very different.

There were swords on the wall, a wardrobe stood across from the foot of the bed. To her left were gossamer curtains that opened out onto the balcony, while to her right was a dresser with an array of various crowns resting atop faceless wooden mannequin heads. One mannequin had no crown atop it, leading Neph to guess that whoever ruled here must be wearing it.

Then she became aware of her ghostly other self, standing patiently with her hands crossed before her. "Come," she beckoned.

Obediently, Neph followed and as her other self gestured toward the door, she opened it.

Then, her astral self led her out into the hall. Neph knew the layout of the palace by heart. From here the throne room was to her left. She followed her other self in that direction, but as she emerged into a throneroom filled with music and ranks of dancers as courtiers and petitioners milled about, whom she saw sitting on the throne caused her to look on in disbelief.

For, the pharoah of Khalatet was Nephthesit, daughter of Akhumet.

She wore the blue kherpesh crown that pharoahs wear during times of war, a wide golden collar, and a linen tunic bound about her waist with a golden belt decorated with lapus lazuli.

The Neph that sat upon the throne spied her entry from across the room, and held out her hand. The music, the dancing, all other activity in the room stopped, and the pharoah rose to face herself.

"You?" the queen asked, "how can you be… *here* when I am already here?"

"I don't know," Neph replied. "How can you… I mean *I* be pharoah?"

"I took the pharoah's throne upon the death of Ammon," the queen responded as she approached her.

"And why do you wear the war crown?" Neph asked her other self.

"We are *always* at war now," Nephthesit replied as she walked past her younger self and gestured for her to follow.

The queen folded her hands behind her as she led Neph out of the throne room the way she came. "After revealing the truth of Pharazon's confession to the council, the Confederation fell apart. The pharoahs make war upon one another constantly now. The traditionalists seek to rebuild Pharazon's empire and rule over it, each hoping to eclipse the majesty of the first Pharoah. Reformists like myself seek to band together and build a new Confederation but mistrust runs deep, and even my closest allies keep their distance out of respect for my might."

"It has been 3 years since I revealed Pharazon's confession." The queen continued as they ventured up the hallway, and Neph followed her back into the bedroom. "3 years of endless fighting. The people of Khalatet... they look to me for leadership... it is *exhausting*."

"Actually, they look to me for more than leadership," she said once the door had been slid shut behind them. She walked across the room, and removed her blue crown of war, placing it upon the wooden mannequin head. "They also look to me to provide them inspiration... to provide them a figure to worship... I have become the very center of their lives."

Then Nephthesit turned and faced her, and in the eyes of her other self, Neph saw a strange look as a smile spread across her face.

"I… I don't understand what you're saying," Neph responded.

"Here, let me show you," she said as she walked toward her, driving her back until her back was against the wall, and then planted her arms against the wall on either side of her, pinning her against it.

Then suddenly… inexplicably, the queen leaned in and planted her lips on the mouth of her other self, dragging her tongue across the inside of her mouth. Neph pressed against the queen, but she wouldn't budge. She resisted the push as she continued to kiss her.

Finally, the queen drew back, disengaging from the sudden lip lock and looking her in the eyes. Neph stood there staring back, afraid and completely confused by what was happening.

The queen reached down and grabbed her younger self's inner thigh, running her hand upwards from there under the hem of her tunic. But before she could go any further, Neph skittered out of her grasp.

"Who gave you permission to touch me?" Neph demanded. She stood there, holding the hem of her rough tunic down over her hips like it was the only thing protecting her chastity. Perhaps in that moment it was.

"I am like a goddess to these people," the queen replied. "But they have all placed me up onto an impossibly high pedestal, and none of them will touch me. I am a woman in my prime. I have reached 22 standard pharoanic cycles, and on all of Khalatet, I can neither find a man nor a woman who will be my lover. I burn with desire. Come. Help me quench my flame. You are *me* afterall. You *must* understand!"

"Who even are you?" Neph responded, retreating from her. "I don't see myself in you at all! What decisions have you made to lead you to this?"

"I have made *so many* decisions; done *so many* things. I have compromised, but they were all for the greater good. I had hoped that *you* might understand…"

"Oh I understand," Neph responded. "I have become Pharazon. In revealing his lies, I have gotten them all over myself and they have consumed me."

Hearing these words, Nephthesit the queen pouted and drew back like a child sensing she was about to be berated by her parent.

"I came here to see the fate that awaited me if I chose to reveal Pharazon's confession," Neph went on, "and now that I have seen it, I want nothing more to do with it. I am ready to leave!"

And with those words, the room suddenly faded into darkness as reality warped and twisted all around her, and Neph suddenly found herself in a terrible sandstorm.

The blowing sands were thick. They battered her form stinging her as they blew against her, and she raised her hands to try to protect her eyes. Through the violent blowing winds, Neph spied a cave before her. She pushed through the storm and reached the mouth of the cave. As she did so, she spotted a figure inside.

It was another her once again. She sat in the center of the cave, with an array of holographic menus open all around her. She wore a pair of tan coveralls, almost exactly like the ones she saw Torgo wear, and on her shoulder, Neph spied the same patch that both Torgo and Tristain wore, displaying the logo of KoloaCorp.

"Who's there?" the other Neph called, raising her hands to shade her eyes so she might see through the glare. As Neph advanced into the cave.

"It's me," Neph replied as she clearly came into view, "well... *you.*"

The other Neph gasped and rose to her feet. Stepping forward, she took both of Neph's hands in her own, and inspected her with her eyes as if to look for any defect that might betray that this Neph was somehow less than real. "How... can you be *here?*"

Neph thought to explain how She had come here to see what she might become, but she didn't know what choice that *this* version of herself had made yet. "It's complicated," was all she said. "I see you work with Tristain and Torgo?"

A wide smile spread across the other Neph's lips. "They are my crewmates… my family. We roam the galaxy exploring new worlds like this one. I have seen… *such wonders.*"

"You sound as if you are happy," Neph responded.

"I am," the other Neph answered. "After I revealed Pharazon's confession to the Pharoanic Council, pandemonium erupted, and we had to make our escape. The Confederation splintered into factions: traditionalists and reformists. They have been fighting a pointless civil war ever since, and both sides hate my guts. We've had to dodge a few bounty hunters and assassins here and there, but…"

"But?" Neph prompted.

"I wouldn't trade the experiences I have had along the way for anything. Space is big. There are plenty of places that are not part of the Pharoanic Confederation where we may hide."

"Where are they now?" Neph asked, "Tristain and Torgo?"

"Torgo is coordinating from aboard ship," the other Neph responded. "Conditions like these can be treacherous for him without his hydropack, which he keeps misplacing. I just spoke with Tristain over the holocom. He is out there somewhere. He says he has found shelter from the storm. We have no choice but to wait until it passes. But tell me, younger sister, and no avoiding the question this time? How did you come to be *here*?"

"I placed my hand into the well of astrum as commanded by my ghostly self. She has brought me here to see the possible fates that await me," Neph responded.

"So you have found the scarab then?" the other Neph asked.

Neph nodded in reply.

"Well," the other Neph replied, "I know nothing of any other possible fate that might have awaited me, but for my part, I am largely satisfied with mine. Choose wisely, younger sister, and choose well."

"I will," Neph responded as they released hands and she stepped back toward the mouth of the cave, and then turned to face the storm. As she did, it completely escaped her notice that the other Neph behind her raised her hand quickly to her lower belly as she felt a kick from within, and a warm maternal smile spread across her face.

And reality faded to black, shifting once again and twisting around her...

Chapter 7

The Past

The weird swirling darkness faded, and I found myself standing in a place I had never been before. I was in front of a building with a sign above the door that read Thornton Petrochemical. Behind me was a parking lot, and beyond a curving coastline highway with a placid sea that lapped up against the sandy shoreline. The skies were blue, the climate was relatively pleasant, and I could taste the salty brine on the wind.

"Where... how?" I began.

Then I spied the ghostly version of Neph standing beside me.

"You stand on Earth, more than a century in the past," she explained. "The man who runs this company is your great grandfather, but then you already know that don't you, Tristain Thornton.?"

"I don't go by that name," I corrected her. "There is too much blood on it."

She nodded, then turned on her heel and walked quickly past me toward the front door of the building.

We walked past the lobby, and waited for the elevator. As I pressed the button, a couple of women in business suits wandered up and waited beside me. One of them looked over to me and smiled. If she was able to see the astral ghost standing beside me, she said nothing.

Finally, the elevator doors parted and we entered, riding the elevator as it made its way up. As we got off on the top floor, the ghost of Neph led me one direction as the two women went the other way. We came to a desk with a middle-aged woman in a grey business suit with a crimson shirt and cravat. She had hazel-colored eyes and hair that was starting to show some grey at the temples.

She was busily typing on her keyboard and did not look up for a long moment. I stood and waited patiently.

"Are you here to see Mr. Thornton?" she asked me. I nodded, noting that suddenly the ghost of Neph was nowhere to be seen. That was a neat trick, disappearing at will.

"And you are?" she asked.

"Varix," I replied. "Tirstain Varix. I represent KoloaCorp. I work for its resource management division."

"Oh," the receptionist replied. "Let me see if he has any availability at the moment." She picked up the telephone handset and started speaking over it.

"Let me show you in, Mr. Varix," she said after hanging up the handset.

She opened the door to his office. The choking stench of cigar smoke filled the room. My great grandfather was a heavyset man with round hanging jowls like the cheeks of a bulldog. His brown hair was receding and greying at the same time, and he wore a black pinstriped business suit that was perfectly tailored, and quite voluminous.

"Mr. Thornton," the receptionist began," this is Tristain Varix representing KoloaCorp."

"All the way here from Hawaii are you Mr. Varix?" my great grandfather began as he stepped in toward me, offering his hand. It was fat and meaty, and I shook it as I was expected to do.

"Yes," I nodded, lying, "Hawaii."

The receptionist moved to leave.

"Ms. De Long," my great grandfather called, "stay."

"Yes Mr. Thornton," she replied in a robotic fashion.

"So Mr. Varix," my great grandfather began, "what can I do for you?"

"Well, cards on the table there, *Roger*," I replied, reading his first name off the nameplate on his desk, "I'm your great grandson from more than 100 years in the future, and I came from a lot further than Hawaii to ask *how dare you*?"

"What?" my great grandfather replied as his cigar almost fell out of his mouth.

"How dare you use up the resources of this planet, and then blast off into space leaving millions of people like your good secretary Ms. De Long here to die on a world that is burning itself up more and more each year? See, I'm alive today because that was precisely what you did. And do you know what? You and yours did blast off into space and successfully founded a colony, but then you left your garbage and pollution everywhere you went, and trust me when I say to you that there are powers out there in the galaxy who don't appreciate that kind of behavior. In my time, we can probably count the total number of human survivors on one hand.

He looked at me incredulously. "You come into my office claiming to be my great grandson and talking to me about polluting the galaxy? Are you crazy? Ms. De Long, call security to escort this man out!"

"No Mr. Thornton," she replied. "I don't think I will."

"What?"

"I've worked for you for almost 15 years, she explained. I have seen you make shady deal after shady deal, each one more ruinous to the planet than the one before it, and I have kept my mouth shut. Why? I told myself that I had 3 hungry mouths to feed. Since we haven't seen my deadbeat ex-husband, I have to do it by myself, and to be able to do that, I needed to retain steady reliable employment, but the real truth is, I was a coward. I kept my mouth shut and I did the job you hired me to do because it was just easier to keep this job than to go out and find another one. I knew that helping you was hurting the environment, and would eventually hurt people, so I stuffed my conscience down because I was afraid you would fire me. But look around you! All the water is starting to dry up! Less water doesn't just mean that we don't have anything to drink, it also means less food can be planted, and that people will starve! And you just want to keep going on like its business as usual, making more deals and stripping the planet bare until there's nothing left? Do you even care about anybody aside from yourself? I don't think you do, and that's why I am tendering my resignation, effective immediately."

My great grandfather's eyes narrowed on her. "Fine, I'll call security myself and have you both thrown out!"

I got to my feet, and as he picked up the handset, I reached out with two fingers and depressed the "hook."

"No, I don't think you will, Rodgy old boy," I said. "See, I never wanted to use the name Thornton. Do you know why? It's because it's got too much blood on it. Billions of people are going to die. People just like Ms. De Long here, and then I will have to live with having that blood on my conscience, and I never asked for that. It was a consequence of your stupidity."

Then I pulled my blaster pistol with my other hand, and pointed it at his forehead. "So you have a choice, *Rodgy*. You can suddenly find it within yourself to acknowledge that there is more to life than profits and the world doesn't revolve around your corpulence, or I can pull this trigger right now and put a hole in your head."

Then Thornton put down the phone handset, and I reset myself so I was now grasping my blaster pistol with both hands. He looked at me and a malevolent smile spread across his face as his brown eyes burned up at me with loathing in them.

"You want to shoot *me*, Mr. Varix? With that popgun? Did you get that out of a box of cereal? If you really are my great grandson, you must know that if you murder me. You will cease to exist."

"Hmm," I replied as I lowered my weapon, and my eyes shot up to the ceiling, in mock consideration of what he had said, "I see you're point. Let me counter with this."

Then I pulled the trigger, and snapped off a shot. A blast of lased plasma shot out of the barrell of my weapon and left a nice burn in the carpet, less than an inch from my great grandfather's foot. My grandfather jumped back, and began panting as he placed his hand over his heart. His cigar fell out of his mouth and rolled across his desk, the burning end scattering embers about. That shook him. It shook him good.

He lunged out and grabbed the cigar off his desk before anything caught on fire, then he mashed the burning end into a well-used ashtray.

Once he had done that, he found the business end of my blaster pistol waiting once again to stare him in the face.

"Now about this other claim you made," I said, "I believe my grandfather is already alive. If he were to inherit your business and still follow in your footsteps, it's still conceivable that he might also blast off into space, just like you did, in which case, the continuity of my existence might not be in any danger at all, but even if he doesn't... even if I am never born, one life is a small price to pay for the future of the Earth and the billions of people who live on it."

"You would sacrifice yourself for people you have never even met?" my great grandfather asked incredulously.

"That's right," I replied. "See, I used to think just like you. Always looking out for myself, always chasing after a payday. But something happened along the way that changed me. Do you know what that was?"

"It was when I found out that the payday I was chasing was actually a person," I replied. "You think you've got it all figured out, right? You've made this economy, this huge freaking machine of perpetual profits that is supposed to make you richer every year than you were the year before, and you force people to buy into the economy. If they want to survive, they have to consume. But then, when you find out that the economy is causing harm, that's not your fault is it? That you blame on the consumers. You try to shift the responsibility of pollution onto them, You tell them that if they recycle it will save the planet, But then you vastly underfund those recycling efforts while each year, you amp up production leading to even more pollution. If somebody complains, you tell them if they don't like it, don't participate in the economy. Not only is that nothing but disingenuous deflection, it's also completely impractical, but it does what you want right? It shuts down further conversation. And all the while you grow richer and richer as people continue to suffer. Even if they wanted to unplug from the economy, even if they wanted to disconnect from your evil that not only harms the planet but exploits children and impoverished workers in poor countries they can't. This whole thing that you have built is too big, and it's banal and… *evil.*"

"You come into my office talking to me about good and evil?" My great grandfather responded. "Listen boy, this is a place of business. Good and evil have no place here!"

"And therein lies the problem," I shot back. "When you pursue profits to the exclusion of all else do you know what that makes you? A parasite. You are a parasite feeding on the fatted ass of humanity… at least for now, until one day you will feed too much and kill your host."

Hearing this, my great-grandfather's eyes grew wide. I could already hear him gearing up with an argument about how he was essential to the functioning of this economy, how he provided jobs and prosperity, and blah blah blah. I decided I wasn't in the mood to go down that rabbit hole of suppressed wages, paying nothing in taxes, or government subsidies and handouts, so I continued before he could respond... "Of course, if you really had the vision and business acumen you claim to have, you would see that there are still opportunities here. There is a way you could make a profit while still doing your part to save the planet."

Thornton sighed and his shoulders slumped as he looked down at the burn mark in the floor, and shook his head. "Well, you're the one holding the gun to my head. What is it you're asking me to do?"

"Take some responsibility," I replied as I lowered my weapon and slipped it back into its holster. "You and yours should be making investments into research and development to invent new technologies that will mitigate the damage, instead of spending money, time, and valuable resources corrupting politicians so that they will obstruct any meaningful progress. Like I said, there are things more important than money. In this age of unparalleled greed, the company that understands that will stand out. Think of the potential profits there are in doing the right thing when nobody else is. You would become an industry leader in green ethical energy production. Think of the PR," I finished with a smile.

My great grandfather looked off into the distance and he nodded. Then he threw up his hands like a film director. "I can see it now, Thornton. We care about *you!*"

Then my great grandfather's attention turned to Ms. De Long who was still standing in the back. "Ms. De Long, you have worked for me for almost 15 years, and you have been an excellent assistant. If I commit the company to making this investment into research & development, and reposition it like Mr. Varix suggests, will you rescind your resignation and continue working for me?"

"It would be my pleasure to, sir," she replied with a nod.

"Well hell, I'll do it then," my great grandfather said, turning his attention back to me. "It's too bad you won't be born for a century yet, my boy. You might make a halfway decent executive. Even I've been known to say that sometimes you have to hold a gun to somebody's head just to get their attention, although I've never actually done it literally!" he said with a nod as he took out another cigar, and sliced the end off. "So tell me," he continued, changing topics, this payday that became a person on you, it seems like your fighting awful hard for her. I assume it's a woman, of course. I respect that. She must be something really special."

"I... I..." I stammered in reply, having not really put the matter into concrete thought until just now, "I think she just might be."

"Trust me, my boy, if you find somebody like that you've got to grab hold of her and never let her go, because you may never find another like her ever again!"

I said my goodbyes and Ms. De Long showed me out. As I boarded the elevator, the ghost of Neph reappeared beside me.

"So, I'm still here..." I responded. "Obviously my great grandfather still blasted off into space."

"He did," Neph responded. "But he also took your advice to heart. He pivoted away from oil and transformed Thornton Petrochemical into Thornton Energy. He repositioned his company into alternative energy production, became a major supplier of solar panels and other solar technologies, and the top player in the drive to hydrogen technologies."

"But climate change still couldn't be averted?" I asked.

"It could not," Neph responded. "The efforts of a single company were not enough to sway the course of inevitability, I'm afraid. One other thing that did change, however, was your great-grandfather himself. He learned to love people more than profits. When he left the planet, Ms. De Long and her family accompanied him.

"Well good," I responded. "At least I can feel better about my family's role in all this. And at least I know we tried to fight the good fight, even if we didn't win. That means something... to me if nobody else."

"So what are you?" I asked as we continued to descend, "Ghost of a future Neph?"

"I am a manifestation of the astral well," the ghostly version of Neph replied.

"So the well is sentient?"

"Oh yes," she explained. "Astrum is alive. It is the composite lifeforce of all living things, and the well is not only sentient, it is conscious, and possesses a will of its own."

"And the well wanted *me* to… what? Travel back in time? to talk my grandfather into not contributing to the destruction of our homeworld?"

"The astrum responds in kind to what is already in your heart," the ghost replied with a smile, "But what's really going to get your gears spinning later on is whether you really traveled back, or if this was all just in your imagination."

Then as I heard the ding of the elevator doors opening, everything grew dark and swirly as reality was suddenly spinning all about me…

…And then once again, I stood in the gallery with the ghostly image of Neph before us. I had my Neph… er… not *my* Neph, but the *real* Neph by the shoulders, and I released her as her own consciousness returned to her at the same time while Torgo looked on.

"You have seen the paths that are open to you, Nephthesit, daughter of Akhumet," the ghostly astral version of herself began. "Perhaps your way has been illuminated for you?"

Neph turned and looked toward me, and she smiled. "It has," she replied.

"And *you* Tristain Varix, have seen the time of generations passed," the ghostly version of Neph said to me, "have you made peace with what you have seen?"

"I have," I replied with a nod as I stood next to Neph.

"Then may both of you be true to the decisions you have made," the other Neph said finally. Then she seemed to dissipate into the mists, and was gone.

"What happened?" Torgo asked us.

"I... she..." Neph began, but she didn't seem like she could find the right words to explain.

"Trust me," I replied to Torgo with a smile as I stepped up beside Neph. She looked over to me, and I looked back at her, "you wouldn't even believe us if we told you."

"Torgo's head swiveled back in frustration as his shoulders sagged. "Aw don't tell me you both had like weird dreamy and visiony time and I didn't get to have any! Why don't I ever get to do any of the fun stuff?"

"Why do you assume it was 'fun stuff?'" Neph asked. "Two-thirds of my visions were *not* 'fun stuff!'"

"Wait!" I protested as we turned and walked on past the well and began our ascent, "You got to have three? How come I only got to have one?"

Chapter 8
The Escape

We continued on our way along the path, and it started to climb once again.

"So what happened back there?" I asked Neph as we began the slow ascent that we assumed led to the way out. "What were your three visions about?"

"She showed me three possibilities born from three choices I could make," Neph replied. "I encountered three different versions of myself. And after experiencing those encounters it has become clear to me that there is only one choice to make."

"What's that?" I asked her.

"I am going to go to the meeting of the Pharoanic Council, present the confession of Pharazon, and that will be that. I will not seek my father's throne."

"Oookay," I responded, "although it seems to me being Pharoah is living the good life. Still, you would have to deal with that nasty bugger back there first *and* his minions, so maybe it's not such a bad idea to walk away..."

"Ammon is just like all the rest of the pharoahs," Neph replied. "He is consumed by his pursuit of power. But power is an empty illusion. It doesn't matter. All feeding the hunger for power creates is more hunger. I was expected to follow my father to the throne, and I wanted to follow in his footsteps, but the self that I met that returned to take my father's throne was miserable. I don't want that. How can I value truth if I am not first true to myself?"

"Well, I get that. After all, if it were up to the rest of the galaxy, I would have already faded into nothingness with the rest of my species, but instead, I decided I wanted to press against the boundaries, and see where that might take me. It sounds kind of like you're doing the same thing. So if you are *really* wanting to go to Kemet, I suppose Torgo and I could give you a ride there," I offered.

"I accept, thank you," she replied. I had this strange sense from her tone that she somehow expected me to make the offer.

I shot Torgo a wordless look of confusion, and he looked back at me and shrugged.

"Just then we heard an all-too familiar voice calling out behind us. "There they are!" Ammon cried as he and his entourage descended down toward the gallery while we were climbing out the other side beyond it. "Kill them!"

"Run!" I cried as Ammon's soliders opened fire once again. Both Torgo and I pulled our weapons and began firing back as we retreated.

As the path continued to climb, we could feel our heads clearing as the astral effects of the gallery seemed to fade all around us. Waving my hand, I found that the holographic menus from the *Menuqet* were available once again.

Up ahead of us, I could see a set of carved pillars decorated with hieroglyphs that marked the border between the caves and a carved corridor beyond that led to the way out.

"Torgo!" I cried, "Get Neph and the scarab to the ship and get her to safety!"

"What about you?" Torgo shouted back.

"Don't worry about me!" I responded. "I'll be right behind you!"

As we reached the pillars, I stopped as Neph and Torgo ran onward.

I Waited there as Ammon, his goons, and Kakuet all ran up the path toward me.

"This is as far as you boys go," I called out as they approached. "End of the line."

"I should have thought you would have learned from our last encounter," Ammon replied, "you dance with a cobra, you feel his fangs."

"I never learn," I responded. "It's part of my charm."

"Appropriate words for the last son of a dead species," Ammon shot back.

"Yeah, you're right," I responded. "We humans got greedy. We grabbed for too much and it cost us everything, but here's the thing you don't get about us; we never stop fighting, because our weapon is hope. You can kill a man, but you can't kill his hope."

"I suppose then I shall just have to content myself with killing the man," Ammon responded, a sadistic smile spreading across his face as he faded to the back of the group. "Shoot him."

Obediently, one of the guards fired and his beam punctured me, burning through the left side of my chest. My eyes widened as I felt the pain and my mouth hung open as I dropped to my knees and then curled down to the ground.

Triumphantly, Ammon strode forward to view his handiwork. "Fool," was all he said. But as he came to stand before me between the pillars, there came a loud beeping noise in tandem as the two pocketfuls of Tetronium beads I had mounted on the pillars activated.

With a loud crash and a wave of choking dust that rolled forth the pillars collapsed on top of us both, and Ammon screamed as he was crushed beneath their falling weight.

Then I came stalking out of the shadows on the exit side of the collapsed pillars and nodded with satisfaction. "No, *you* were the fool, Ammon," I said. My holographic self had done his job, and done it well. The passage was completely closed off with Kakuet and Ammon's goons blocked on the other side, leaving them with no other option but to go back the way they came. This of course meant that Neph, Torgo, and I were free to make our escape.

I let Torgo and Neph know what had happened, found the passage out and made my way to the ship. We blasted off leaving that dying world that was once the homeworld of my people behind us.

Kakuet, true to his word had the payment rescinded from my account.

3 days later, we were on Kemet. Neph had made all the appropriate arrangements and was scheduled to address the council at the Forum of the Prophets.

"How do I look?" She asked as she approached. She wore a wide golden collar decked with rubies and lapus lazuli, a fine linen sheath wrapped tightly around her form torso to ankles, golden bracelets and anklets, and a gossamer cape that hung from the collar.

"Beautiful," I replied.

Hearing this she smiled.

"Are you ready for this?" Torgo asked.

Neph turned and nodded to him once.

Then the curator of the forum poked his head in. "It's time," he prompted. Neph followed him out on the stage. She held up the scarab for all to see and... well, you already know the rest. Bedlam followed as the Pharoahs turned on one another. The revelation of Pharazon's confession sparked an 11-year civil war. At this point, you might be asking who won? Wrong question. The real question to ask is this: does anybody ever win a civil war? The answer is no, but there are always plenty of losers until the killing finally stops.

That evening, after Neph, Torgo, and I had made our escape from the chaos on Kemet, Neph sat on the bridge of the *Menuqet* still dressed in fineries.

"So," I began as I entered the bridge and came to stand in the aisle between her seat and the one across from it, "you found the scarab of truth, and you presented it at the Pharoanic Council. What will you do now?"

"For the first time in my life, I honestly don't know," Neph replied.

"I was hoping you would say that," I responded as Torgo came in carrying a roughly Neph-sized set of KoloaCorp coveralls.

"Why not consider flying with us?" I asked. "The pay is terrible but the commissions are good, and you'll never starve. I could always use another resourceful hand."

I stepped aside as Neph rose, walked over, took the coveralls from Torgo, and clutched them to herself. She turned to face me.

"I didn't exactly make any friends on Kemet today," she began. "What about assassins? bounty hunters?

"You'll be part of the crew," Torgo replied. As Neph turned back to face him, he elaborated: "Crew looks out for each other."

"That's right," I added as Neph turned again to face me. "Whatever they send, we'll deal with it."

"Then I accept," she said with a knowing smile.

Also from Brett J Baker:

- The Freeworlds Chronicles
- Song of the Multiverse
- The Neamhain Prophecy
- Twilight Realms Online

royalcrownpress.com

www.ingramcontent.com/pod-product-compliance
Lightning Source LLC
Chambersburg PA
CBHW050538160726
48003CB00002B/657